A Night Out

A Night Out

A Short Story

Queen McPhillips

Queen McPhillips

CONTENTS

CONTENTS

We'll Be Back

"Be good," they say to the young child as they kiss her on the head and walk downstairs. Thirteen year old Daniel could care less as he plays on his video game.

"D, you're watching your sister while we're out.", his mom says.

"Yeah, okay. Fine.", he remarks, without taking his eyes off the game.

"We'll be back.", they say as they walk out the door. The clock strikes ten as 6-year-old Mya struts down the stairs.

"Where's mom and dad?", she asks with a glimmer in her eyes.

"They're out, now hush!" he yells.

"I'm trying to beat my high score!"

"Okay I'll be quiet", she replies, "but only if you play a game with me!" she exclaims excitedly. He glares at her then smiles slightly as he looks out the window.

"Okay I got it. Let's play hide and seek!"

"Oh I love hide and seek, can I hide first?", Mya asks insistently.

"Of course," he replies eagerly, "but the only rule is that you have to hide outside!"

"Don't want it to be too easy now do we.", Daniel says in a snarky tone.

"But D, it's so dark!" she whines pointing out the window.

The sky was so dark, you could barely even see the moon. They watched for a moment as the branches seemed to scratch at the night.

"Well I guess we aren't.."
"NO!" she interrupts running out the door, "start counting!"
"I will." He laughs as he locks the door and sits back down to play his game.

2

He'll Never Find Me Here

Looking for places to hide, she runs through many different spots until she sees a tall corn field in the distance. She runs to it thinking of how long it will take him to find her. As she stops at the field, she feels the cold wind blowing through her hair. She feels a rising desire to turn around when she hears a faint, "Ready or not, here I come!"

She darts through the stalks, pushing through anything she sees and when she finds a dry spot, she sits down to wait for him to find her.

He'll never find me here! *I'm guaranteed to win!*

She sat thinking of all the fun times she's had with her brother as the wind began to pick up.

As the frosty ground rubs against her bare skin, she curls up with only her nightgown and a few leaves to protect her from the midnight air.

This Isn't Funny

Time seemed to drag on waiting for him to find her. The longer she lay waiting, the sleepier she became. The warmth of the leaves and the comfortableness of her night clothes began to lull her into a deep sleep. Her slumber is swift and short as she is soon jolted awake by a voice calling out to her.

"Mya, Mya, Mya!" It starts to get louder as the whispers turn to screams. She stands up and she sees a tall haze moving through the wheat field.

She can't make out what it is so she decides to walk towards it and investigate.

"This wouldn't be the first time Daniel's played a prank on me and it definitely won't be the last.", she thought cautiously approaching the gleaming unknown.

"Daniel, this isn't funny!" she says.

"You're scaring me!"

She approaches with uncertainty until she is right next to it. She sizes it up trying to make out what it is. It seems to look like Daniel beholding the same ripped blue jeans and grey hoodie he had on earlier. Although she couldn't see the face, she knew her brother's stature.

"Why would you do that?", she says through small sniffles.

"You know what mom and dad said about scaring me like that! It's really mean you know!"

Out of nowhere, the being begins to laugh hysterically. She can't help but stumble back; she never expected him to act like this. This is too much, even for a joker like him. Her senses take over as she runs away from the devilish sound.

It slowly turns around and begins pursuing her; it's bones snapping and cracking with every step it takes.

"Come to Daniel!" It yells, getting faster with the sound of the crunchy leaves being pulverized beneath it's weight.

She runs faster and starts screaming but it's as if no one could hear her. She increases her speed as the stalks whip across her one by one. All the running starts to get the best of her and she stops to take a breather. It is quiet, there's no more crunching or snapping. Just the sound of the wind slapping against the trees. She turns around to see if it was still coming after her, but when she turns back around, she trips over a rock and everything goes black.

Daniel, Is That You?

When she woke up, all she could hear was the sound of water trickling. She could smell the burning of something but she wasn't sure what. She blinked quickly, trying her best to open her eyes, as they burned harshly. The beads of sweat blurring her vision, she rubbed them trying to clear them. After a few minutes of quiet, she heard footsteps approach her. She saw a figure emerge from the darkness. She shivered at the thought of who or what it might be.

"Would you like something to drink?", the voice of her dad began to speak. She was so thirsty. Her tongue dry and her mouth longing for a sip of anything.

"I have your favorite. Orange juice, all you have to do is drink it.", said the voice as it walked closer to her waving a cup filled with juice in her face. Scared and reluctant, she denied it.

"I said, do you want something to drink?! It's yours, drink it!", it exclaimed in a voice deeper than anything she's ever heard before. It felt as if it could swallow her up at any moment. She watched as she felt the hatred and malice explode through it's makeshift body. The voice guttural and raspy, it became louder and louder.

"Answer me now little girl! You don't want to make me angry!", the voiced yelled switching between voices she's heard before.

"Just do as you're told and drink the damn juice!"

First her dad, then her mom, then her brother, and back to the deep voice again. Over and over it would switch, mocking her, until she couldn't take it any longer.

"No," she screamed. "You're not who you say you are!"

She lifted her head as she opened her eyes wide to see. Her vision started to give way and she saw something she never could prepare for.

The creature who wore her brothers clothing held a face of wickedness. It's body became elongated and dark; boney but sturdy as if it could pick her up with no effort at all. It's face was nothing like she had ever seen before. It looked just like Daniel. But also nothing like him. It changed continuously into something so evil, it made her want to burst into tears. Her brother's face began to melt off revealing it's true nature. The creature bore a huge set of sharp yellow teeth worse than any animal she's ever seen. It's smile viscous and taunting, it yelled, "You're right, I'm your worst nightmare!"

It started to laugh viciously once again as it shoved a rag over her face. She was then met with the most overwhelming emotions. Her eyes began to water and she started to feel dizzy. Her legs shook and her feet started to tingle as if pins were stabbing into them. Her heart was pounding and she felt the breath slip from her lungs.

5

That Wasn't Me

She opened her eyes with a gasp and looked around. She found that she was still in the cornfield and began to panic. Looking down at her body, she noticed there were burns and bruises all down her body and her night clothes were ripped. She heard someone yelling her name again.

"Mya, I'm coming!"

"Stay away!", she yelled wanting nothing to do with whoever she was talking to. The voice got closer and louder. She huddled in the stalks hiding her face in her legs and began to cry.

She was then picked up in the arms of her brother, who yelled, "Why are you down here?"

"You know you're not supposed to come to the corn field now. It's still dark out and why are you bruised, what happened to you?!"

"I've been here all night Daniel! I don't know what happened but why didn't you come looking for me?", she said through sniffles.

" What are you on about? There's no way you were out here. Last night you came banging on the door and I let you in and then I tucked you into bed!", he exclaimed over her tears. Her jaw dropped when he said those things but he didn't give her time to speak.

"Close your mouth girl. Oh, mom and dad called. They won't be home until later tomorrow.

"Also, we need to talk about you doing that creepy stalking thing. What was that about?", he asked with annoyance and confusion in his voice.

She raised her eyebrows at him weirded out by his statement.

"D, what are you talking about?"

"Oh come on Mya. It was early in the morning and when I woke up you were standing over my bed staring at me with a weird smile on your face. You ran away before I could say anything. It wasn't funny you know."

Her stomach drops as he describes his encounter.

"D, something's in our house!", she says jumping from his arms and sprinting back home.

6

Imposter

She reaches the house and flings the door open. She bounds up the stairs with her brother close behind her. He's going on and on about how she needs to calm down but she can't hear him. She turns her room upside down making sure it was still in her possession. After coming up empty-handed, she let out a sigh. She walked over and gave her brother a hug.

"It's okay D, we're safe now."

"You're crazy My. I don't know what you're on about but you need to relax", he says, "I'll run you a bath".

She had just enough energy to muster up a grunt as she plopped on her bed and buried her face in the blanket. With all the "fake sister" excitement, she soon dozed off. Before she knew it, her brother was shaking her awake to help her into the bath.

As she got into the bath, they started to talk. Whatever was going on had brought them ten times closer and allowed them to bond. Daniel always loved his sister but he wanted to do his own thing. He always hated having her little shadow follow him around. But looking after her showed him maybe Mya wasn't so bad after all.

"I'll be right back, I'm gonna go get you a towel", he exclaims as he walks out of the bathroom.

She closes her eyes and tries to relax but can't get the vision of that monster out of her head.

Maybe she was crazy and she really was inside the whole time.

"It was just a dream. A really REALLY bad dream."

She put her head under the water in hopes of making her worries go away but when she came back up, a girl that looked just like her was staring back at her slowly walking towards her and laughing like a maniac.

Her eyes began to glow red as her ankles snapped the opposite direction. Within seconds, she rushed Mya, grabbing her by the hair and shoving her under.

She tried and tried to push her off but she couldn't breathe. The more she tried to sit up, the harder she was pushed under. After what seemed like forever, she popped up and jumped out of the bath crying her eyes out.

Daniel ran back in the room and picked her up.

"What's wrong?", he kept asking but she couldn't do anything but cry.

As the boy carried her out of the room, she looked back at the mirror where she saw her alternate self glaring and smiling wickedly back at her waving and mouthing the words, "He's next".

Safe Haven

He tries his best to comfort her but it seems like nothings working. Hours go by before she stops crying and by that time, it's night again.

"Can I sleep in your bed tonight?" she asks through watery eyes.

"Sure, but only until mom and dad get home.", he replied.

She went to go get her stuffed animal and climb in bed, but when she came back, Daniel was gone.

She started to freak out as he returned from the bathroom.

"Shhh, It's okay, I'm right here. Let's go to sleep.", he said as they climbed into bed. Normally, when they lay together she has to ask him to hold her, but this time, he did it himself. He cuddled up to her and rubbed her back, soothing her to sleep. Just before her eyes closed, she felt a soft kiss on her head and heard him whisper I love you. Something she hasn't heard him say in a long time.

"I love you too. You really are a great brother.", she replied soaking into his warmth and drifting off to sleep.

Intruder

Their soft slumber was interrupted by wild alarms blaring throughout the house.

"Stay here!", he yells running downstairs with a bat.

As he disappears from her sight, she hears boisterous footsteps coming back into the room. She tries to hide under the blanket but it is ripped off and she sees herself once again.

"You made it out last time. This time, you won't be as lucky!", she raves as her head turns a whole 360 degrees while her bones cracked and popped as if she had broken every bone in her body.

All of a sudden, she flips backwards and begins briskly crawling towards her laughing maniacally.

"Leave me alone!" she yells, but her words are caught in her throat by the girl taking a bite out of her leg. She holds on with her teeth and won't let go.

She couldn't take it as the girl ripped through her leg with her nails and chewed off the remains. Mya screams out in pain and tries to kick her off but she isn't strong enough.

Blood is squirting everywhere and she is starting to feel sick as she yells for her brother.

He runs back upstairs in shock.

"What are you yelling about, it was a false alarm! No one's inside My."

"Daniel, my leg, its bleeding!", she yells watching the blood run off the bed and drip onto the stuffed bear and all over the blanket.

"What are you talking about Mya?", he says confused as he inspects her leg, "there's nothing there."

9

Invisible

She watches as her alternate self starts to walk backwards smiling mischievously, taunting and mocking her.

"D, please tell me you see this!", Mya yells as her leg burns intensely, the missing flesh bubbling with blood.

She looked for a solace, any type of assurance from her brother. But instead, he says nothing.

"Daniel, look at me! Why aren't you saying anything?", she exclaims as tears well up in her eyes. It's as if something shut off in his head, his face shooting up at hers.

She called out but it was as if nobody was home. His face in a daze and his eyes almost clouded over, he stood looking through her.

"Why can't you hear me? Stop ignoring me! I need you D!" Mya watched as he sat on the bed and put his head in his hands.

"I wish I never let her outside. My baby sister.", he exclaimed through sobs, "I just wanted a few minutes alone to play my game. I never meant for her to get hurt. It's all my fault! If I could only be with her one last time.", he declared breaking into uncontrollable blubbering.

Mya walked up to him and placed his hands on his arm.

"Bubba, I'm right here. Why can't you see me?" As he felt her arms on his skin, he stopped in his tracks and became silent.

"I can feel her. She's still here, my baby sister. I hope you know that I always loved you.", he bawled as he spoke.

Mya tried to make sense of what was going on, but it was all so confusing.

"Mya, if you can hear me, I wish I would've played hide and seek with you. I mean actually played instead of ignoring you like I did. It was my pride keeping me from it, but I didn't mean for this to happen. I wish I could take it all back. I never wanted anyone to hurt you, I just wanted you out of my hair for a few minutes.", he states disheartened,

"Please sissy, forgive me."

10

Lost Then Found

Mya runs down stairs, tears trailing behind her. She finds a crumpled newspaper sitting on the table. Looking past the tear drops rubbing off the ink, she reads...

6 Year Old Girl Found Missing in Corn Field. She Was Found With Chunks Taken Out of Her Leg, Several Broken Bones, And Dozens of Cuts And Bruises. It Looked As If Animals Had Gotten to Her. Found Wearing A Tattered Nightgown Drenched In Blood. Laying Next To The Body Was A Rag Laced With Chloroform And A Half Drunken Cup of Orange Juice Poisoned with Ammonia. Cause of Death: Aspiration in Lungs.

"No, this is a lie! I'm alive, I just know it!", she screams throwing the paper to the floor. She runs back to Daniel who had gone into her room and sat on her bed holding her favorite doll and sobbing.

"Tell me you can see! I'm here aren't I?"

"Bubba, I'm here! Stop crying for me!", she yelled in his face.

But to no avail. He continued to cry for a bit until his voice was hoarse and his face was red as if it was going to burst.

"I love you sissy. I'll see you again someday.", he states wiping his face, kissing the doll and tucking it into bed.

He then walks through Mya and closes her door.